Ant
Invasion!

With special thanks to Mariam Vossough

To my goddaughter, Amy M

First published in paperback in Great Britain
by HarperCollins *Children's Books* in 2009
HarperCollins *Children's Books* is a division of HarperCollins Publishers Ltd,
77-85 Fulham Palace Road, Hammersmith, London W6 8JB.

Visit our website at: www.harpercollins.co.uk

2

Text copyright © Working Partners 2009
Illustrations copyright © Duncan Smith 2009

ISBN-13: 978-0-00-731041-8

Printed and bound in England by Clays Ltd, St Ives plc

Ant
invasion!

JOE MILLER

Illustrated by Duncan Smith

HarperCollins *Children's Books*

Spinner's Wood
is full of sticky mud, tall trees
and long grass. But most of
all, it's full of bugs! Now, some
people think that bugs are pests.
But they haven't met Gonzo or
the **Bug Buddies** – four best
friends called **Zap**, **Buzz**,
Lurch and **Crunch**. Their life
would be perfect if it wasn't
for a spider called **Spinner**,
who has eight legs and one
mission: to trap the whole wood
in his evil web. But you'll
soon find out that even
bugs can be heroes...

Contents

CHAPTER 1

Zap flew beneath Crunch, feeling
tinier than ever next to the giant
stag beetle. His antennae twitched
nervously as he looked at his friend's
antlers. He could get squished at any
moment! Crunch was a big beetle
with a big problem – he was rubbish

at flying. Gonzo the wise old grasshopper had been teaching them some flying techniques, but Crunch still had a lot to learn. Zap hoped his friend wouldn't wobble into him!

"Try to keep your antlers still when you fly," Zap reminded him. He held his breath as Crunch headed down towards Rotten Row. *Please don't crash-land,* he thought. Crunch zoomed in close to the ground and stretched out his wings for balance. Yes! Crunch managed

to land without falling flat on his face.

"Well done," cried Zap. "All that flying practice is starting to pay off."

"Thanks," said Crunch, huffing and puffing.

Buzz the ladybird landed on a crumbling tree trunk.

"Why does Gonzo make us practise so hard?" he said. "I'm pooped."

"Did someone say **poo?**" cried Lurch, flying down to join them. "I need a new dung ball."

Lurch the dung beetle thought about poo **all the time.** Zap reckoned he even dreamed about poo!

"I need a snack," said Buzz. "Flying always makes me hungry."

Zap hovered in the air above his three friends.

"We'll eat after Web Patrol," he

said. "We promised Gonzo we'd
keep an eye on Spinner's webs."

Spinner was Zap's biggest enemy.
The giant spider wanted to take
control of the wood – and he'd stop
at nothing to get his own way.

"We haven't seen Spinner for
days," said Lurch. "Perhaps we've
scared him off."

"Spinner wouldn't give up that
easily," said Zap. "He's sure to have
something else planned and—"

Zap didn't have time to finish his
sentence.

"**Woo-aahh!**" came a cry from above.

He looked up to see Guy the gadfly speeding towards him. Zap flew quickly out of the way, as Guy landed on his back next to Buzz.

"Looks like someone else needs some flying practice," laughed Lurch.

Guy rolled over and jumped up
blinking his large, shiny green eyes.

"Hi guys," he said, speaking really
quickly. "Why aren't you at the
moving-in party for the yellow ants?
They're setting up home beneath
one of the acacia trees on the edge
of the wood."

"What yellow ants?" asked Zap,
frowning. There had never been any
yellow ants in Spinner's Wood.

But Guy had already sped off
again. "Can't stop," he called over
his shoulder. "I'm heading back

15

there now. The food is **yummy
scrummy!"**

"Let's go to the party!" cried
Buzz.

Zap laughed. "I thought you were
tired."

"I'm never too tired for party
food," replied Buzz.

Zap smiled at his excited friends.
"Web Patrol first and then, party.
Deal?" he said.

The Bug Buddies flew off on their
rounds. They checked on Spinner's
favourite webs. But they were either

completely destroyed or full of
holes. Zap hovered in the
air before a torn web
that was covered in
dirt. Buzz came up
beside him.

"Perhaps that's why the ants have moved in," said Buzz, as they gazed at the ruined web. "Because Spinner has moved out. The wood's safe again."

"I hope that's true," replied Zap uncertainly. "But Spinner has lived in the wood his whole life, would he really just leave?"

Lurch flew up beside them. "Stop worrying," he told Zap. "Spinner's gone, it's a beautiful day and we've a party to go to!"

Zap wanted to do one last web

check, but his friends were already heading off. He flew after them, taking a final look back at the raggedy web.

Had Spinner really left the wood for good?

CHAPTER 2

It wasn't hard for the Bug Buddies to find the party. They just followed the sound of excited laughter echoing off the trees.

"It sounds like a **buzzing** party," joked Buzz.

They landed beneath the acacia

tree and a yellow ant immediately

rushed over to them.

"The famous Beetle Ball champions!" he cried. "I've heard all about you."

Zap's antennae pricked up in surprise. "How come?" he asked.

"You've only just arrived in Spinner's Wood."

"We've been talking to some of the bees," said the ant, pointing a leg upwards.

Zap glanced up to see a group of bees hovering in the blossom of the acacia tree. "They don't usually collect acacia pollen," he said.

"We told them to try it – it's scrumptious," the ant hurriedly explained. "Would you like some of the extra-sweet honey they've made?"

"I thought you'd never ask!" said Buzz, pushing his way to the front.

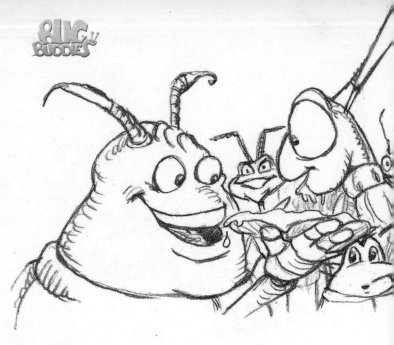

The ant led the Bug Buddies into
the party. The place was packed
with so many insects, Zap had to try
hard not to get trodden on!

"Here you are," said the yellow
ant. He gave each of them a flower-
petal bowl brimming with acacia

honey. Zap lowered his head and

took a sip, but the honey was *so*

"No more for me."   sweet it made his

stomach ache.

Zap watched

as Buzz, Lurch

and Crunch slurped up

25

the honey greedily.

"Can we have some
more?" Lurch asked,
holding out his
empty flower petal.
Crunch and Buzz
were both licking the last
of the honey from their lips.

Zap looked around. "It's weird
seeing yellow ants in the wood," he
muttered. "They normally live in the
meadow and stay underground."

Buzz shoved his face into another
bowl of honey. "I'm glad they're

here," he mumbled

between mouthfuls.

"This is the most

delicious thing I

have ever tasted!"

Zap found a twig to sit on,

away from the crowd. *I'm the only*

bug not eating honey, he realised as he

looked around.

As the party continued, the Bug

Buddies started acting a bit crazy.

Lurch had found a new dung ball,

which he'd covered in honey – and

now he was stuck to the top of it,

27

being pushed around by a group of

giggling earwigs.

"Faster! Faster!"

Zap knew Lurch would never normally treat his dung balls like that.

Meanwhile Crunch was having an arm-wrestling competition with an over-excited frog beetle.

And Buzz was challenging everyone to count how many spots were on his shell. If they lost, he got to eat their honey!

"Everyone's out of control," Zap muttered to himself, climbing off the twig. He pushed his way through the party and noticed something else. He had been wrong – he *wasn't* the only bug not eating honey. He could see that the yellow ants weren't tucking in either. They stood around the edges of the crowd. And Zap didn't like the thin smiles that lit up their faces. The ants looked almost smug.

But they were just harmless little bugs… right?

CHAPTER 3

Zap shook his head, clearing it of
doubts. *I'm just being silly,* he thought.
Lurch is right. I worry too much.
*It's not the ants' fault the bugs have
eaten too much honey.* Zap looked up
at the clear blue sky and noticed
how low the sun was.

Oh no... They were late for Beetle Ball practice!

Zap flew back to gather his friends. His little wings drooped when he saw Crunch snoozing under a tree root. Lurch had also crashed out still stuck to his dung ball and Buzz was snoring loudly next to him.

Zap took a deep breath and shouted as loud as he could. **"Wake up!"** he yelled. "Gonzo's waiting for us."

Crunch was the only one to move, groaning and rubbing his eyes

with his claws. Together, Zap and

Crunch managed to wake up Lurch.

But, although he flapped his shiny

wings, Lurch couldn't get off the

sticky dung ball.

His wriggling made it roll into

Buzz, jerking him half-awake.

"Want... more... honey..."

mumbled Buzz, before falling straight
back to sleep.

Zap shook his head. "We've never
been late for practice," he said.

"Why don't you and Crunch go
on ahead," suggested Lurch. "I'll
wake Buzz once I've got unstuck."

Zap didn't like leaving his friends,
but he didn't see any other choice.
He and Crunch flew off to meet
Gonzo at the practice clearing.

Crunch was so tired, his flying
was wobblier than ever. Zap's wings
quivered nervously as the bugs

landed beside Gonzo. The wise old grasshopper looked stern.

"You're late," he said.

Zap quickly explained about the yellow ants' party. And how much honey his friends had eaten.

"Yellow ants?" Gonzo repeated, frowning. He looked round as the final two Bug Buddies flew towards them. Lurch landed clumsily, his wings still sticky from the honey. Buzz came down with a thud at Gonzo's feet.

"And what have you two got to

say for yourselves?" said Gonzo,

glaring at them.

"I don't feel well," moaned Buzz.

Gonzo shook
his head,
unimpressed.

"It's too late

for Beetle Ball practice now," said

the grasshopper. "But tomorrow, I

want you to find out exactly what

those yellow ants are up to. Since

when did bees need help finding

pollen?"

"That's what I thought," said Zap,

quietly. But Gonzo was already hopping away.

The Bug Buddies settled down for the night beneath the leaves of a bog bean plant. Zap was relieved that his friends were finally back to normal.

"I feel really bad about letting Gonzo down," said Buzz.

"Me too," said Zap. "We'll make it up to him tomorrow."

"That honey did taste amazing though," said Buzz, as he drifted off to sleep.

Zap pulled a leaf around his tiny body. He thought about what Gonzo had said. He was right – those ants were up to something. How did they know so much about acacia pollen? And since when did they care about honey?

Zap's wings shivered as he looked out into the darkening wood. Something strange was going on, and it was down to him to find out what it was.

CHAPTER 4

Zap opened his eyes and watched

the morning sun climb over the

treetops. He stretched out his six

legs and turned to look at his

friends. Crunch was snoring loudly,

Lurch was dribbling in his sleep

and Buzz was...

Gone!

Zap's tummy did a nervous flip –
something was wrong. Buzz never
went anywhere this early – not
without breakfast!

He shook Lurch and Crunch
awake.

"Perhaps Buzz has gone to
apologise to Gonzo," suggested
Crunch.

The Bug Buddies flew over to
Gonzo's Rock. Zap's heart sunk as
he spotted the old grasshopper was
alone, munching on some leaves.

There was no
sign of Buzz.
They landed
next
to Gonzo and
Zap told him
what had happened.
"You should check with
those yellow ants," he said. "He
might have been tempted by the
thought of more honey."

"Not after it got him into so much
trouble yesterday," protested Zap.

"Buzz is a good little ladybird,"

replied Gonzo, "but his head is easily turned. Especially when there's food involved. **Now, go!**"

Zap was full of worries as they flew over to the yellow ants' nest.

"Watch out!" cried Lurch.

Zap looked round to see a blur of yellow and black flying towards him. It was Stripes the bumble bee, who was crying so much he couldn't see where he was going. Zap zoomed

out of the way, doing a loop-the-
loop to avoid being stung.

"Are you OK, Stripes?" he asked,
flying after his friend.

The bee shook his furry head.

"The acacia honey has been
stolen!" he replied. "We worked so
hard yesterday and now it's all gone!"

A loud cry came from behind
them. Zap looked round to see a
frog beetle fly out of a tree.

"It can't be all gone!" he wailed.
He lost control and bounced into a
knobbly branch, before plummeting

"Noooooo!~

to the ground. Zap and the Bug
Buddies looked at each other.

"Everyone's going mad for that
honey," said Crunch.

"Everyone except the ants,"
buzzed Stripes.

**"That's what I thought
yesterday!"** cried Zap. His mind

whirled as he pieced together the clues. "The ants must have known that all bugs would love the extra-sweet acacia honey. That's why they were so keen for everyone to have some. And why they didn't eat any themselves."

"Some bugs will do **anything** for more of that honey," gulped Lurch. "And Buzz is one of those bugs!"

"But why would the ants do this?" asked Stripes, bobbing in the air.

"Someone must be giving them orders," Zap said. "And who do we

know who's great at giving evil

orders? **Spinner!**"

Crunch shuddered with fright.

Zap hovered in front of them,

flapping his wings.

"Stripes, you fly back to your hive

and alert the bees," he said. "Lurch,

you go and tell Gonzo what we've

learned. Crunch and I will track

down the ants."

The Bug Buddies split up. Zap and

Crunch flew further into Spinner's

Wood. They soon spotted lines of

scurrying yellow ants, each one

carrying a small leaf smeared with a drop of acacia honey.

Zap's eyes widened. Nearly every bug in the wood was trailing after the ants!

"Where are the ants leading them?" he said.

"Wherever it is, it won't be good," replied Crunch.

The trees were taller and the air
cooled as Zap and Crunch followed
the line of ants to the edge of
Shadow Creek.

"**Help!**" cried a voice up ahead.

"I recognise that voice," said Zap.
"It's the frog beetle."

Zap flew towards the cry,
Crunch's claws clattering nervously

behind him. He peeped out from

behind a leaf to spot the frog beetle

struggling to break free from…

"A huge web," gasped Crunch, as he flew up beside Zap. It was stretched right across the entrance to Spinner's territory. Which was exactly where the ants with their honey trail were heading…

The bugs were being led into a TRAP!

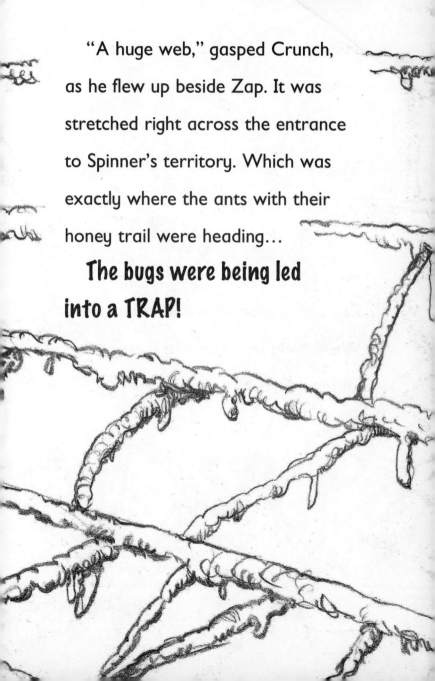

CHAPTER 5

Zap's tiny heart thudded in his chest.

Webs hung across every tree in

Shadow Creek.

"The ants are using the acacia honey to lure bugs right into Spinner's lair," he said. "The insects are so desperate for the sweet taste, they don't notice they're flying straight into his webs!"

Crunch was trembling. "It's like a giant b-b-bug trap."

"And I'm totally trapped!" yelled the frightened frog beetle.

Zap and Crunch flew over to him. Crunch cut the beetle free, even though his claws were shaking.

"You should have brought Lurch

with you," Crunch said. "I'm rubbish at being brave."

"You're braver than me," said the frog beetle, flying away. "I'm getting out of here!"

Suddenly, the leaves around them began to sway and a loud buzzing filled the air. A swarm of bees arrived in a shimmering cloud of black and yellow.

Below them, Lurch pushed a dung ball along the ground, while Gonzo hopped beside him.

Zap flew down to the ground as everyone grouped around the wise grasshopper.

"Spinner hasn't left the wood," announced Captain Drone, the leader

of the bees.
"He's still
here, and he's
attacking each
and every one of
us. What should we do?"

"Zap, Crunch, Lurch and I will each
lead a patrol of bees into Spinner's
lair," said Gonzo. "With stinging bees
on our side, we've got a better
chance of defeating him." Gonzo's
large eyes clouded with sadness.
"And let's not forget that our friend,

Buzz, is in there somewhere."

Zap felt his stomach churn. He hoped his spotty friend was OK.

Gonzo began to organise the bee patrols. Zap drew Lurch and Crunch into a huddle.

"Whatever happens, we must work as a team," he said, "just like when we're playing Beetle Ball."

Lurch nodded in agreement, but Crunch looked more nervous than ever.

"I can't lead a patrol," said Crunch. "My flying is too wobbly."

Zap touched the tip of his wing on Crunch's shoulder. "Just do what Gonzo taught you," he said gently. "And remember, you're braver than you think."

"Yeah," said Lurch, flapping his wings encouragingly. "Go, Bug Buddies!"

The patrols lined up round the edge of the creek. Gonzo gave the signal. It was time to go! Zap zoomed up and over the first web, the bees humming

loudly behind him.

The sunlight disappeared as they

flew into the dark heart of Spinner's

realm. Glistening strands of silk

covered almost every part of Shadow

Creek. A giant maze of webs

stretched from branch to branch.

Zap took a deep breath and

began to weave his way through

the webs. His little

wings skimmed the

silky strands.

Thank goodness for all the flying practice Gonzo made us do, he thought.

Zap finally saw an opening in the trees up ahead.

"Keep going," he shouted to the bees. "We're almost through!"

The bees followed close behind

as Zap broke out into a clearing.
The air was filled with a sickly,
sweet smell. Zap looked down to
see a gigantic lake made from
acacia honey! He almost dropped
out of the air in shock. The lake
was full of bugs, who waved giddily
up at Zap.

Some were slurping the honey, some were sleeping and some were stuck at the edges of the pool.

As Zap scanned the lake for Buzz, he caught sight of his reflection. Suddenly, an enormous, black shadow loomed behind it...

Zap's heart pounded as he glanced up to see Spinner hovering above him.

"Welcome," the evil spider hissed.

CHAPTER 6

Spinner's sharp fangs glistened in the sunlight. "Let me guess," he said, "you've come to rescue these greedy beetles?"

Zap held his head up high – determined not to show how frightened he was. "Yes, I have," he replied defiantly.

"Not this time, little weevil," said the spider. "Say goodbye to your bug friends – **they're about to take a journey into my stomach.**"

Zap heard a sound. A faint buzzing… and rustling leaves. The other patrols had arrived! He had to stop himself from cheering out loud as he spotted his friends taking up positions around the lake. Luckily, none of the ants – or Spinner – had noticed them. But as he glanced over the lake of honey, Zap saw a yellow

ant dragging a dozy bug towards
Spinner. A red and black bug...

Buzz!

Zap zoomed towards his friend.

"Where are you going? Get back
here!" cried Spinner. But Zap pulled
his wings in tight and rammed his
body into Buzz's captor. The ant
dropped Buzz and fell on to his back.
Zap crashed to a halt next to him,
landing awkwardly on his wing.
The ant's black legs waved
frantically as he spotted the bees
heading towards him.

"Oh no! I don't want to get stung!" he yelped. He rolled himself upright and ran over to the other ants.

Zap got to his feet, trying to ignore his sore wing. All around, the bees began attacking the ants, swooping down low and exposing their sharp stingers.

"Go, bees!" Zap cried. He watched Spinner retreat quickly to the safety of one of his webs.

Zap crawled over to check on Buzz.

"Yucky poo-poo," mumbled his friend, still half-asleep. He was safe for now.

Zap sniffed the air. What was that awful smell? Zap looked up to see a speeding dung ball rolling

towards them! He only just managed

to dive out of the way as... **BLAM!**

The ball of poo

crashed into a

group of ants,

sending them flying

through the air.

"Sorry Zap,"

shouted Lurch,

from the other end of the

lake.

"It's OK," replied Zap.

"Good shot!"

The yellow ants raced up the hill,

back to their home beneath the
acacia tree. Zap watched them
scurry away – then spotted
the last yellow ant crawling
over to Buzz. The ant gave
him a hard shove, sending
him rolling towards the lake.

"**BUZZ!**" shouted Zap, as the
ant scurried away up the hill.

Zap raced forward and grabbed
one of Buzz's legs. But Zap was tiny
and the ladybird was heavy. Buzz
was beginning to sink into the lake
of honey.

"**Let go!**" shouted Crunch,
landing near Zap. "I'll handle this."

Zap managed to drag himself
back to the bank. There was a wet
sound as Crunch pulled Buzz out of
the honey with his enormous antlers.

"What are you doing?" Buzz
mumbled sleepily. "I was having a
nice lie down."

"Thanks," said Zap, relieved that
Crunch had been able to help. "Can
you get him out of here?"

"Sure thing!" said Crunch. He
gently held sleepy Buzz in his antlers

and flew over to a hiding place in a tree stump.

Time to deal with that evil spider, thought Zap. He looked at the chaos around him. Bees were still grappling with ants and Gonzo was dragging drowsy bugs to safety. How was he going to get to Spinner past all this? Then Zap spotted an underground tunnel in the grassy bank. He crawled towards it and plunged into the muddy darkness, hoping it would take him underneath the fighting insects — straight to Spinner! It was dark and damp beneath the ground, but Zap forced himself to keep moving.

As he flew up back into the light it took a moment for his eyes to adjust. Then he saw Spinner grinning down at him from his web.

"Here comes lunch," sang Spinner. The spider raised up his body on his thick black legs, ready to pounce.

CHAPTER 7

"**Wait!**" shouted Zap. "I can fly really fast. **Aren't you too old to catch me?**"

Spinner's eyes filled with anger. He dropped down from his web on a strand of silk, with his legs reaching through the air towards Zap.

"I'll never be too old to catch a pesky little weevil!" he said.

Zap darted out of the way, flying up and over the spider. He noticed that the strand Spinner was hanging from was thinner than usual. A plan started to form in Zap's mind. *If I can make Spinner even angrier*, he thought, *I might just get the better of him.*

"Maybe you're not too old to catch me," shouted Zap, **"you're just too fat!"**

Spinner swung his body round, desperate to catch hold of Zap. "Come here," he snarled.

"Too old! Too fat!" teased Zap.

Spinner gave another desperate heave, trying to swing himself closer to his prey. Zap noticed the thin silky strand start to weaken under the weight of the giant spider.

This is my chance, he thought.

Zap zoomed above Spinner and bit down hard on the sticky silk.

"Aaahhh!" cried Spinner, as the strand snapped and he plummeted

down towards the lake.

Zap watched as – **PLOP!** – the

spider's hairy body fell right into

the honey.

Spinner struggled furiously as he

tried to clamber out. His legs circled

through the air and his teeth
gnashed. "Get me out of here!" he
cried. But no one moved to help.
The more he struggled, the quicker
he sunk into the sticky gloop until –
SLURP! – Spinner disappeared
beneath the lake.

Zap flew down to the grass,
excitedly.

"I always knew Spinner would
come to a sticky end," said Lurch,
rolling his battered dung ball.

Captain Drone hovered in the air
above the lake.

77

"That's the last acacia honey we'll be making," said the bee. "It's back to our usual lavender pollen from now on."

"Glad to hear it," said Gonzo, hopping over to join them.

Zap saw Crunch emerge from the tree stump where he'd been taking care of Buzz. Behind him, Buzz was lying on his back, still fast asleep.

"And here comes the beetle who said he

wasn't brave," said Zap, proudly.

Crunch gave a modest smile. "I did what I had to," he said.

"Yippee!" cheered Lurch. "The Bug Buddies saved the day!"

"The bees and I will stay and make sure everyone's OK," said Gonzo. "You three get Buzz home. He's had quite an adventure."

Zap winced at his sore wing as the Bug Buddies flew back through the maze of webs. He took one last look over his shoulder at the pool of honey. Spinner was nowhere to be

seen. It was hard to believe that it
would be the last he'd ever see of
that mean spider. But at least they'd
managed to stop his evil plans for
today.

CHAPTER 8

Back at the practice field, Buzz
finally woke up.

"How do you feel?" Zap asked.

Buzz rubbed his tummy. "A bit
queasy. But not too bad," he said.
He began to lick the last of the
sticky honey off his legs as Lurch

tried to repair his dung ball. Crunch
was cleaning his antlers on blades of
grass.

Gonzo flew down to join them.

"Are all the other bugs OK?"
asked Zap.

"Everyone's fine. It looks like you
picked up an injury, though," Gonzo
said, nodding at Zap's damaged
wing.

"It's nothing," Zap shrugged, not
wanting to make a fuss.

"I'm sorry I let you all down,"
Buzz said quietly. "I wanted to make

up for what happened yesterday. So,
I got up early to go and see if I could
figure out what the ants were up to.
Only, they started offering me honey
and then…"

"You made a mistake," said
Gonzo, softly. "But you're not the
only one."

Zap, Crunch and Lurch
exchanged awkward glances.

"You thought having fun was
more important than your
responsibilities," he continued.
"There's nothing wrong with

enjoying yourselves. But no one can have fun if the wood isn't safe – and it's your job to help make sure it is."

Zap's antennae drooped. Gonzo fixed his gaze on him. "But I have a feeling that a certain little beetle realised all wasn't well. Perhaps next time, he should speak up more."

Lurch turned to Zap, a sheepish look on his face. "We should have listened to you, Zap," he said.

"We will in future," said Buzz.

"Promise," added Crunch.

Zap ducked his head, embarrassed, but secretly pleased that Gonzo knew he had tried to do the right thing.

"And I promise to be a bit more bossy next time," agreed Zap.

"Not too bossy," Lurch warned him. All the Bug Buddies laughed.

Zap looked past his friends, above the swaying trees to the yellowy-orange sun setting over Spinner's Wood. *But is there going to be a next time?* he thought. *Spinner is gone — isn't he?*

"**Come on!**" cried Lurch,
launching himself into the air. "**Let's
celebrate!**" As Zap flew up,
following his friends in a huge loop-
the-loop, he knew that there would
be more challenges ahead, as they

fought to protect Spinner's Wood.
But he'd be ready. And his Bug
Buddies would be by his side every
step of the way.

BUG FACTS

LADYBIRD

NAME: Buzz

FAMILY: Coccinellidae

SIZE: 6 mm

HOME: flowering plants
of Spinner's Wood

LIKES: eating, spitting at bad
bugs, his spots

DISLIKES: bugs who can count,
Lurch's dung balls, Web Patrol

BUZZ

Ladybirds may look pretty, but Seven-Spots can be fierce. If attacked, they squirt their own blood at their attacker, which is stinky and bright yellow!

They hibernate in groups and can be spotted piled on top of each other to keep warm.

BUG BUDDIES

Tunnel Trouble

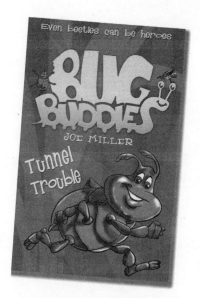

A storm is coming and scary tiger beetles need shelter. But can the Bug Buddies trust them? And is Spinner really gone for good?

OUT NOW!

Turn over for a sneak preview of book four...

Zap tingled with excitement as he hovered above the starting twig. Wizzy the horsefly was lined up next to him, buzzing.

"OK," said Crunch, the stag beetle. "First one to Gonzo's Rock and back wins. **Ready... steady...**

GO!" Crunch swiped his antlers down.

The race was on!

Zap flapped his wings with all his might. Spinner's Wood became a green blur as he sped around the rock. He may be just a tiny weevil, but he felt as tall as a tree when he was flying.

Zap did a loop-the-loop as he soared across the finish line. He'd won! *I'm the fastest bug in the wood, he thought. Maybe I'm the fastest bug ever!*